Starring Sammie . . . as the girl who becomes a big
fat liar (but whose pants *don't* catch fire)

Starring Alex . . . as the girl with the voice of an
angel (who can be a little devil too)

Starring Jolene . . . as the runaway who's trying
to do a good turn (just make sure
she doesn't turn on you)

Starring Brody . . .

. . . as the model from the States
(who's in a bit of a state herself)

Helena Pielichaty
Illustrated by Melanie Williamson

OXFORD
UNIVERSITY PRESS

OXFORD
UNIVERSITY PRESS

Great Clarendon Street, Oxford OX2 6DP

Oxford University Press is a department of the University of Oxford.
It furthers the University's objective of excellence in research, scholarship,
and education by publishing worldwide in

Oxford New York

Auckland Bangkok Buenos Aires Cape Town
Chennai Dar es Salaam Delhi Hong Kong Istanbul Karachi
Kolkata Kuala Lumpur Madrid Melbourne Mexico City Mumbai
Nairobi São Paulo Shanghai Taipei Tokyo Toronto

Oxford is a registered trade mark of Oxford University Press
in the UK and in certain other countries

British Library Cataloguing in Publication Data available

ISBN 0-19-275248-0

3 5 7 9 10 8 6 4 2

Designed and typeset by Mike Brain Graphic Design Limited, Oxford

Printed in Great Britain by Cox & Wyman Ltd, Reading, Berkshire

to my niece Louisa Lotte Pielichaty
who is nothing like the niece in this story!

with love

Welcome to
ZAPS

Contact: Jan Fryston NNEB (Supervisor)
on 07734-090876 for details.

Please note: Mr Sharkey, headmaster of Zetland Avenue
Primary School, politely requests parents/carers <u>not</u> to
contact the school directly as the After School Club is
independent of the school and he wants it to stay that way!

All children must be registered before they attend.

Zetland Avenue Primary School (ZAPS) After School Club
Newsletter

Dear Parents and Carers,

We have lots of exciting things planned for this year and hope you will tell your friends and neighbours all about us. Children do not have to attend Zetland Avenue Primary School to come to After School Club; any child is welcome as long as they are aged between five and eleven and have been registered.

Special Events:

1. November: **Children in Need Fundraising.** We will be joining in with the main school's activities. We wonder what Mr Sharkey will be getting up to this year? (If you remember, last year he sat in a bath of smelly jelly!)

2. February half-term holiday: **Film-making Week.** Media Studies students from Bretton Hill College will be showing us how to make and star in a real film. Watch out, Hollywood!

3. Easter: **Pop Kids.** We will be staging a talent show to perform in front of parents and carers.

4. Summer: **Get Active!** Summer Sports activities for everyone throughout the holidays.

Also: ⟫E-PaLS⟪

Once the new computers have been installed we are hoping to set up an Internet connection to After School Clubs throughout the UK. Children who are interested will be able to write to their 'E-pals' from Penzance to Pitlochry!

See you all soon,

Jan

Jan Fryston (Supervisor)

After School Club

Sammie Wesley

Reggie Glazzard

Alex McCormack

Lloyd Fountain

Mrs Fryston
Supervisor

Mrs McCormack
Assistant

Brody Miller

Sam Riley

Jolene Nevin

Brandon Petty

Some comments from our customers at the After School Club:

'It's better than going round my gran's and having to watch Kung Fu films all day in the holidays'—

Brandon Petty, Y1

'It's good because I am home-schooled so the After School Club gives me a chance to mix with children my own age and make new friends.'

Lloyd Fountain, aged 9

'I love going to ZAPS After School Club— there's so much to do. It's a blast.'

(Brody Miller, Y6)

— You feel at ease
— On the purple settees
— The staff are kind
— And help you unwind
— So come along
— You can't go wrong

— (Sam Riley, Y5)

'After School Club is OK, apart from the rats and poisonous biscuits.' (Don't worry folks – just messing with your minds – Ha! Ha!)

Reggie G. aged 133*

*our resident comedian informs me he prefers to use months to describe his age – JF

'There's not nowhere better than After School Club and I like Mrs Fryston because she is kind and understands how you feel about things.'

Sammie Wesley Y5

'I've been to other After School Clubs before but they've been rubbish and I've always been kicked out but this one is the best.'

Jolene Nevin Y5

'I have been coming to After School Club since it started because my mum is one of the helpers. I enjoy the craft activities and when new people start, like Jolene.'

Alex McCormack Y4

What do you think? Add your own comment

Chapter One

Do you have anyone famous in your class? Here's a tip for you if you do. Treat them like any other regular person. That's all they want and, believe me, I should know. Just for the record, my name is Brody Miller and I'm a child model. You would probably recognize me if you saw me—I have been appearing in catalogues and magazines since I was a baby. I am also the daughter of Kiersten Tor, the ex-supermodel turned potter and Jake Miller, the fashion photographer. Sure, we all have a high profile—it comes with the territory, as does the stalker following me around—but stick me in a Year Six classroom and you wouldn't be able to tell me apart from anyone else. Really.

Actually you can cut the 'stalker' thing. It is one

girl at my After School club and 'stalker' is probably not the right word to describe her. I am not sure what *is* the right word to describe Sammie Wesley. All I know is that at three thirty, at the end of school, Sammie would be waiting for me on the top step of ZAPS After School Club. I'm talking every afternoon, rain or shine, hail or sleet, snow or fog, until I got there. No one else; just me. The days I don't come, she doesn't show. I know; I checked with Sam Riley, another club regular she hangs out with. Once we are inside, that is that, she will go off to do her thing, I will go off to do mine. First, though, is always this one-to-one. Tonight was no different.

'I like your boots, Brody,' she began, 'they're well decent.'

'Thank you, Sammie,' I replied, waiting for her to move aside; but I knew she wouldn't. So I waited. Despite the cold February wind blowing round us, she just kept staring at my Doc Martens but not saying anything. I guess they are pretty unusual. They're eighteen-hole DM

2

originals which Mom customized for me—one with a Union Jack design, the other with Stars and Stripes; so my left foot's English like my dad and my right foot's American like my mom. Neat, huh?

Sammie continued to stare at my feet, her hair whipping round her rosy, placid face, still not budging. I figured this greeting ritual with me is something she had to go through, like not treading on cracks in the sidewalk or something. I know from experience she can do odd things sometimes but deep down the girl's harmless so I play along with it. After all, I lived in the States until two years ago. I'm used to weird.

'Do you go modelling in them?' she asked.

I nodded. They had been perfect for the new season's Funky Punk range I had just completed working on. Without giving away too many trade secrets, I told Sammie what clothing style the top guys at Funky Punk would have hitting the high street as soon as Dad finished the shots for them.

'Oh. That sounds dead good!' she enthused. 'I'll tell our Gemma—she loves Funky Punk stuff, though my mum says it's a right rip-off.'

'Yeah, I know what she means—it is way too expensive. Dad hopes his shares will rocket so he can retire and buy a boat.'

My dad's nautical dreams failed to impress Sammie. She seemed miles away, looking at my feet again. 'My mum got some new boots once,' she said.

'Oh?'

'They caused problems.'

'Blisters?'

'No.'

'Oh.'

That seemed to be the end of that but just as I was building up hopes of an early entry into the mobile Sammie looked up and added that my hair looked nice today, too.

'Thanks,' I said patiently, trying not to shiver. Could she not feel this wind at all?

A pained look passed over her face, as if she'd said something wrong and only just realized. 'What I meant was, your hair looks really nice every day but today it looks even nicer than normal,' she explained quickly.

'Thanks,' I said again, 'yours is nice, too. Cool headband.' I like to give a compliment when I receive one. Immediately, Sammie dragged the yellow padded thing off her head and held it out to me.

'It's yours,' she exclaimed.

4

'No, no, I couldn't, really,' I said in alarm. It was stained and frayed round the edges. A little gross, if I'm being honest.

Sammie gazed at me, her eyes wide and eager. 'Please take it. Please.'

'No, really. I'm fully accessorized. Got slides coming out of my ears at home!' I joked but she looked so disappointed and I didn't want to hurt her feelings. Tentatively I placed the headband on my head and smiled. 'How does it look?'

'Nice,' she said shyly. She smiled at me uncertainly but still didn't move.

I squinted past her and through into After School club. It was already busy. I could see Mrs Fryston, the supervisor, setting up the oven in the corner—it is Wednesday, so it's baking day—and behind her Reggie is standing with his hands in his pockets, looking cool, waiting for the computer to load. I used to have a mighty crush on Reggie but since he told me he didn't plan on dating until Year Seven I backed off and just see him as a friend.

'Anyway, girl in a whirl,' I told Sammie. If I hurried, I could grab the other computer but just as I was about to make a dash for it, I felt something hit me over the head. I twizzled round to see Mr Sharkey, our headteacher, grinning up at me. 'Ah! The famous Miss Miller! Give these to the Nut in the Hut, would you?' he said, holding out a pile of letters still warm from the photocopier. 'And tell her, next time I'm charging!' He strode off back towards the main school building, whistling, and I turned round to face Sammie again but she had disappeared. So snow and ice couldn't budge her but the sight of Mr Sharkey could. Go figure.

By the time I'd dumped my coat in the cloakroom, Lloyd Fountain, the home-schooled kid with the eccentric taste in bright-coloured baggy-jumpers, had taken my place at the remaining computer. I sighed heavily and searched round for Mrs Fryston, the 'Nut in the Hut' as Mr Sharkey had so charmingly called her. She was over at the book corner with little Brandon Petty and is not a nut at all—she is a very nice lady.

Tears the size of pear drops were running down Brandon's pudgy cheeks. 'What's up?' I asked, squatting down so I was eye level with him. He's only five.

'Look who's here, Brandon. It's Brody!' Mrs Fryston said over-cheerfully. 'Brandon can't find his favourite book, Brody. He's looked everywhere.'

'It's been stoled,' Brandon sniffed.

'Oh no! Not *Eat Your Peas*?' I guessed, seeing as I had read it to him about three million times. 'Shall I help you look for it?'

'Would you?' Mrs Fryston said gratefully. 'I need to get the biscuit group going.'

'Sure. Oh, and Mr Sharkey gave me these,' I said holding out the sheets.

She smiled and took them from me, a definite blush appearing on her cheeks at the mention of his name. Let me tell you a secret. Mr Sharkey and Mrs Fryston are dating. I only know because I saw them together at Piccollino's restaurant a few weeks ago. They were so busy playing footsie under the table they didn't notice me over in the corner and Mom said there was no way I was allowed to go up to them and say 'congratulations' in case I was jumping to the wrong conclusion. Since then I have been collecting evidence and I have it in spades. For example, Mr Sharkey just happening to 'pop in' on us in the mobile every two minutes. And when he does, I can tell you for a fact Mrs Fryston automatically does the blushing-thing and this is not a blushing-thing kind of lady. No way was I jumping to any conclusions. Even now Mrs Fryston was stroking the top sheet dreamily with the palm of her hand. It's so sweet! 'Oh, good—the letters home about next week's half-term activities. Will you be coming?' she asked me.

'Yeah—'fraid so,' I sighed, coming back to earth with a bump. Mom was tied up with a new exhibition at The Gallery, a kind of arts studio Sam Riley's mom runs above Riley's card shop, and Jake was in London so I didn't have much choice.

Mrs Fryston glanced at me sympathetically, not offended that I so obviously would rather not spend half-term with her. 'Never mind, Brody, we've got something fun planned. Film-making!'

'Cool,' I said. I felt my spirits rise—film-making sounded better than the usual half-term stuff. 'Brandon and I could give these out for you, if you like, while we're hunting for the book,' I offered to Mrs Fryston as an afterthought.

'Would you, Brody? That would really help. Thank you.'

'Oh, and Mr Sharkey says he'll charge next time,' I told Mrs Fryston as she handed me back the sheets.

Mrs Fryston mouthed a large 'oh!' and faked a scowl. 'The cheek of it. He knows full well I have

8

already paid for his precious photocopying!'

'He's just messing with you, Mrs Fryston. You know what he's like.'

'I do! It's a pity he's nothing better to . . . oh, Tasmim!' she broke off. 'Put the flour down. Not yet!'

I took hold of Brandon's hand. 'OK, buddy, let's go find this book.'

'OK, let's.'

'What's it called again? Eat your knees?'

'No. *Eat Your Peas*!'

'Eat my peas?'

'No, *Eat Your Peas*!'

'That's what I said!'

It took a while to find the thing. Brandon asked everyone about his book and then I followed through with a letter home. Neither Sam nor Sammie at the tuck shop had seen *Eat Your Peas*, nor anyone in the book corner, the dressing-up area, the baking bunch, nor the oddballs with the short attention spans who drifted aimlessly round all afternoon.

We spotted the book by chance in the end, sticking out from under a pile of shiny red paper next to Alex McCormack as we passed the craft table. She must have overheard me asking people for the past half an hour but had let us wander around anyhow.

'I'm using it!' Alex snapped at Brandon as he tried to retrieve the book. She glowered fiercely at the poor kid. Another five seconds and he'd turn into a frog.

I glanced at her work. She was sticking lentils and macaroni to an over-glued piece of cardboard. There was nothing in that activity to do with the book at all. No siree. I bet you she had hidden it on purpose because that's the kind of thing she did. For some reason she got a mighty boost from teasing the little ones, especially the boys, which is weird as I heard she had a brother who had died. You'd think she'd be kinder.

Across the table, her mom was pouring lentils into a jar and she glanced up through her straight peppery-grey fringe, then glanced down again. I knew she wouldn't do anything. That was half the problem—Alex got away with so much because Mrs McCormack allowed her to every time. 'We'll bring it back,' I said firmly to Alex and grabbed the book.

'If he loves it so much why don't you buy him a copy? You're rich enough, aren't you?' she muttered.

'I'm not rich,' I told her calmly.

'But you live up Sandal Road in that massive house with a swimming pool,' she replied. 'You must be rich.'

'As I said, I'm not rich,' I repeated, leaning in real close and keeping a cute smile on my face in case her mommie was watching, 'I'm stinking rich.'

With that, I led Brandon to the book corner, snuggled down with him on the purple couch, and read.

Chapter Two

'Good day, Brode?' Mom asked as I climbed into the passenger seat next to her an hour later.

'Ish,' I said crankily. I was still smarting about what I had said to Alex, plus I had English with my private tutor, Mrs Morgan, next, plus history homework from Mrs Platini once I did get home, plus I was hungry. That's a lot of pluses.

'Buckle up, hon,' Mom instructed.

I sighed hard and did as I was told, thinking about the Alex thing. Why had I said that to her about being stinking rich? I know better than to come out with dumb comments like that. Mom and Dad are always warning me not to sound off about possessions.

The Rich Girl tag gets me every time though.

What was I supposed to do? Sleep in a shed? It's not my fault I live in a big house.

'What's wrong?' Mom asked.

'What? Nothing.'

'You just grunted.'

'Did I?'

'Aha. And I haven't had my kiss.'

'Sorry.' I shrugged all thoughts of McCormack out of my head and leaned across to kiss Mom on the cheek. She smelt shower-fresh and was wearing her black sweater, tan suede jacket, and faded jeans. Just how I liked her. 'Tha looks reet neece, Kiersten,' I said, trying to imitate the Yorkshire accent kids like Reggie had.

'Ta, love,' Mom replied, trying to do one back but sounding really fake. Mom's originally from Kansas and it's not an accent you can easily hide.

'Reet neece,' I repeated for emphasis.

'Ta,' she said again, chuckling.

'Too reet neece to be wasting time sitting outside Mrs Morgan's for a whole hour.'

Mom glanced at me and shook her head. 'Nice try,' she said, handing me my snack of Babybel cheese and a banana before pulling out on to Birch Road and heading downtown to where Mrs Morgan lived.

I tugged at the red wax tab on the cheese and grumbled. 'But why do I have to go, Kiersten? I so do not need extra tuition.'

'Oh, honey, you so *do* need that tuition!'

'I so do not!'

'You "so" do or you "so" wouldn't be saying "so" all the time!' Kiersten laughed. 'Besides, you know you have to keep up, especially now you're going to private school.'

'Stupid Hairy Mary's,' I muttered.

'Queen Mary's,' Mom corrected proudly. 'And there's all the time off you've had recently,' she continued. She means with the Funky Punk thing. Dad did kind of ignore school hours during a job. I hadn't put in a full week for a month now.

'Got me there,' I admitted and chewed my cheese instead. Mom drove on, grumbling about her perspex display units not arriving for the exhibition and how she was sure the whole thing was going to be a disaster, until eventually we pulled up outside Mrs Morgan's large terraced house. To cut a long lesson short, I went in, said, 'Hi', to Mrs Morgan, compiled a list of words ending in -ible and -able and other riveting exercises, said, 'So long', to Mrs Morgan then came out again.

'Right, what next?' I asked Mom, climbing into the car. 'Is there a class in Japanese you'd like me to go to? Or a chimney you'd like me to sweep somewhere?'

Mom switched off her Chili Peppers CD and smiled. 'Next, my poor little munchkin, is the station.'

'Yes!' I laughed. The station meant Dad was coming home. He tried hard to get home one night mid-week but never told us when until the last minute in case he couldn't make it.

'And then Piccollinos?' I asked eagerly. One usually went with the other and the pasta at Piccollinos is just the best in the world.

Mom revved the engine. 'Smell that linguini!' she grinned.

Chapter Three

Dad's train was on time. As soon as I spotted him, I did my usual thing of running down the platform and he did his usual thing of opening his arms real wide and swinging me round until I was dizzy. 'How's my beautiful daughter?' he asked.

'Fine. How's my ugly dad?'

'Still ugly.'

'So I see!'

Dad isn't really ugly, though people round here do frown at his ponytail sometimes, as if it's a crime for a guy of fifty to have one.

'What's that trash on your head?' he asked unexpectedly, lowering me back onto the platform.

'Oh,' I said, reaching up and feeling Sammie's headband. Trust him to notice straight away—he can spot a rogue accessory at two hundred metres.

'Someone gave it to me,' I mumbled.

'It's ghastly—take it off. Or better still, lose it.'

Before I could say a word, he'd tossed it into a garbage can near the sliding doors and without a second thought went straight on to kissing Mom. I peered into the bin after it but Dad scowled so hard I didn't dare retrieve it. I glanced behind me at the garbage can and sighed. Sorry, Sammie.

Piccollino's is just up from the station on Westgate. It's a tall, three-storey, red-brick building brightly painted in green, white, and red. Fredo, the owner, was only just opening when we arrived. He shook hands enthusiastically with Jake, pinched my cheek, and gave Kiersten a long hug before kissing her hard on both cheeks. 'Ah! *bella*, *bella*, Kiersten,' he sighed. 'When you gonna leave this no-good guy and come and live with me, huh?'

Kiersten blushed and laughed him off, as she always did when anyone hit on her.

'You tease!' she told him.

The first thing Dad did when we sat down was to throw a flat brown envelope on the table. I grabbed for it eagerly, knowing it would be the Funky Punk contact prints. 'Are they good?' I asked, remembering the hours of posing I'd had to do. Not just me, either—there had been ten of us altogether, messing about in a freezing cold park in Hertford. Jake shook his head. 'They're not bad,' he mumbled.

'Only not bad?' I said worriedly, glancing from one picture to the other. I hoped I hadn't been the one to mess up.

'What's wrong with them?' I asked, passing the proofs over to Kiersten. They looked fine to me.

'They're all clichéd,' Dad sighed. 'I want something with more edge. Brody, you'll need to skip school tomorrow. I want to take some more one-on-one shots.'

I agreed instantly. 'Sure.'

Mom didn't. 'Couldn't you use one of the agency models? India or Marlonne or someone?' she asked.

'You're kidding me! Pay those pompous wannabes when I've got my little home-grown Jerry Hall right here?' He winked at me and I winked back. I liked being his number one choice.

The waitress, Imogen, arrived to check if we needed drinks. I tried for a Coke but I got nowhere as usual. 'Honey, your teeth,' Kiersten and Jake chorused, shaking their heads in unison.

'Water then,' I mumbled while they ordered a beer each. Modelling sucks sometimes. How many eleven year olds do you know who aren't allowed Coke? I mean, it's a staple, right? I'm just glad they didn't see the candy I bought at After School club.

Imogen distributed the menus, dutifully recommending the house special.

'Thanks, petal,' Jake said, smiling at her. She smiled back over-brightly before returning to the kitchen area. 'So, how have my two precious girls been coping without the light of their life?' he began. Before either of us could answer, his mobile rang. Dad saw whoever was on the other end off pronto, with a 'Yeah, yeah, action that, fine, fine. Ciao.'

'Oh, Jake, don't you know where the off-switch is

on that thing?' Kiersten complained from behind her menu.

The quick answer to that is no. Within seconds it was ringing again. 'That man's ears will drop off into his soup one day if he doesn't watch it,' Mom muttered to me. 'What are you having?'

I told her I couldn't decide between spaghetti napoli or the calamari. 'Me, too!' she squealed. We had this freaky thing going where we always chose the same things. Finally we both decided on the spaghetti then turned to Jake, pulling crazy faces at him to make him hurry up so we could order. He waved his hand at us irritably and it was obvious something was wrong. 'What do you mean . . . ' he blurted down the phone. 'What Friday? This Friday? I'm not even going to be here. Kiersten? Sure, but she's—' He then stared at the mobile in his hand in disbelief.

'Who was that?' Mom asked.

'She's hung up!' he said, as if he couldn't quite believe it.

'Who was it?' Mom repeated.

'Claire, who else?' he snapped and decided the mobile did have an off-switch after all.

Chapter Four

Just for the record, Claire is Dad's other daughter from his first marriage to a woman called Lynne. He was only young when he got hitched the first time—about nineteen, I think—and he wasn't married to Lynne for long but it was long enough to produce my half-sister Claire who, at thirty, is only five years younger than Mom. Claire lives in a place called Washington, Tyne and Wear, where Dad originally came from and is a real pain. She's always asking for something over the phone—usually money; or moaning about something—usually her kids. She has a daughter called Jolene, who's a bit younger than me, and two stepsons with her new partner Darryl. I'm not sure of their names—isn't that terrible, not knowing? The thing is, I've only met them once, and that was at Grandma Miller's funeral last year, so it wasn't exactly the best time to get acquainted. Whenever I ask why we don't see them, Mom says it keeps things simple and Dad says everyone's too busy. I think there's more to it than that but know better than to 'go roun' diggin' ditches if I can't fill 'em up again' as my grandma Tor used to say.

'What did she want this time?' Mom asked, tucking a strand of hair behind her ear.

'Apparently she's dropping Jolene off on Friday,' Dad growled.

'Where?' Mom asked.

'At the house.'

'Whose house?'

'Our house!'

Mom paled. 'What? Why? For how long?'

'The week!' Dad said, mystified. 'And I can like it or lump it!'

If I'd dared, I'd have laughed, they both looked so totally put-out. You'd have thought Jolene was an escaped convict or something instead of my ten-year-old niece. 'Claire can't just decide that,' Mom frowned.

Dad held his hands up, palms out, which meant, 'It's a done deal—change the subject.'

'But this week of all weeks! Heck, I can't even look after my own child let alone someone else's!' Mom protested.

'I know, I know,' Dad agreed rapidly.

'Why can't Lynne do it?'

'She's in hospital having her varicose veins out, apparently.'

There was a long pause as they both took distracted sips of their drinks. Time for Brody Bright-Ideas to step in. 'Hey,' I said, 'there's not a problem. Jolene can come to After School club with me. It's great—we're doing film-making. She'll have a ball.  Look.' From my pocket, I withdrew the letter home from Mrs Fryston and slid it across the table. Dad took hold of it first, then passed it on to Mom with a shrug. 'Then in the evenings we can chill out and watch videos or swim if the pool's warm enough or . . . ' I reeled off a list of home-based things we could do that wouldn't cause any hassle.

Dad took hold of the letter and read it properly this time. 'It's an option, Kierst,' he said. 'The club's on from nine to six—that's decent enough—and I'll be home all weekend so that frees you up for the exhibition, doesn't it?'

'Does it?' Mom said, staring into her glass.

'Well, the kid's arriving at seven o'clock Friday night. We don't have much choice, do we?'

'No,' Mom snapped, 'we don't, do we, Mister Assertive.'

Chapter Five

Next morning, Dad and me set off to re-take the Funky Punk shots. We drove to a side street off Jacob's Well Road in the city centre and parked outside an abandoned charity shop whose windows had been fly postered to death. Jake thought it was *the* spot for 'edge'. I was already dressed in all the gear. For those who are interested in fashion, from our spring/summer collection, today's ensemble, apart from my boots, was a crew-necked skinny-fit top teamed up with a short kilt, leaf green denim jacket, and cobalt blue tights. Practical, different but not *too* different, and way too expensive—talk about hitting the market.

It was the details I liked best in this new range, such as the skull-and-crossbones pin through the hem of the kilt. 'Get the pin in, Jake,' I told him as he checked his camera.

'Hold still,' he muttered. Cars passed and people stared as Dad flashed off a million shots. His camera always makes a soft whirring sound as it clicks. I focused on his black leather jacket and wondered what Jolene would be like. It was going to be fun having a relative come with me to After School club. I had made plenty of friends at Zetland Avenue but no one special, you know? No number one best bud. Everyone was already established in pairs by the time I got there in Year Four. I'd enjoy introducing a proper family member to everyone.

'That's it! That's excellent!' Jake effused. 'Smile— show me those beautiful teeth.'

I showed him my beautiful teeth.

'OK, now I want more punk than funk, hinnie,' Jake instructed. In Yorkshire a girl is a lass but where Dad comes from she is a hinnie. 'Here, put these on,' he said, handing me a pair of designer shades.

'Oh, cool!' I said, sliding them on.

'They fell off the back of a Porsche,' Dad joked.

'I bet,' I said. In the space of ten minutes I had to

look angry, sad, mean, angry again, and plain cheesed-off.

'Slump more,' Dad ordered, 'turn sideways, cross your feet.'

I slumped. I turned sideways. I crossed my feet.

Finally, Jake looked up and grinned. 'OK, that should do it. You're a star, Brody Miller! I have never worked with any kid more natural, even if I do say so myself. "Get India or Marlonne." I don't think so!'

I felt myself beaming with pride. Dad doesn't often give compliments but when he does, you know he means them. Between you and me, that's why I keep up with the modelling thing and don't mind missing school. Like when Sammie waited outside the mobile for her one-to-one sessions with me, times like this were my one-on-one with Dad. And they were precious.

I had to change into my uniform in the Happy Harvester Ladies Room nearby then Jake dropped me off at the school gates. 'Thanks, Brode. I'll see you tomorrow night, OK?'

'Yep.'

'You'll be all right now? Do you want me to come in and see Mrs Platini?'

'No,' I said, 'I'll be fine. I've got the absence note you wrote me.'

'OK, and remember, if Mrs Platini gives you a tough time, tell her careers come first.'

'Yeah, I'm sure she'll buy that one.'

Dad did a flashy U-turn in the road and screeched off, pipping his horn a dozen times in farewell. Such a quiet guy.

The afternoon was tough going. Mrs Platini didn't give me a hard time, exactly, but made sure I had a copy of everything she had covered that morning 'so I wouldn't fall *further* behind', which meant I missed break trying to catch up. I also knew I had After School club and another session with Mrs Morgan to survive before I could get home and start preparing for Jolene's visit.

First, of course, was Sammie.

'Hi, Brody.'

'Hi, Sammie,' I said, halting reluctantly by the mobile steps as everyone filed past.

'Your hair looks nice.'

'Thanks—yours too.' I peered closer. Actually, she had done something to it. The colour had changed, from a dull straw to a kind of Day-Glo tangerine. It was—erm—interesting.

Her face reddened as she tried to hide a bunch of dry strands behind her ears. 'I was trying to match yours but I don't think our Gemma got the right box,' she said quietly. 'Aimee Anston says I look like a carrot cake.'

'Well, tell Aimee to take a hike,' I advised, trying to peer over Sammie's shoulders and check out the indoor situation. I could just see Mrs Fryston discussing something with Mrs McCormack. 'Anyway, gotta go.'

'Brody?'

'Yep?'

'You know I gave you that headband yesterday?'

I felt instantly awful as I remembered Dad throwing it away. 'Yep.'

'You couldn't let us have it back, could you? Only it was our Gemma's and she went right into one when she found out I'd took it.'

'Oh—erm—I'll have a look for it tonight.'

That seemed to be all she wanted to hear. She grinned and let me pass.

Chapter Six

The next day, Friday, is usually my short day because I don't have any extra tuition or After School club to go to but I guess because I was so excited about Jolene arriving later on, time stretched further than melted mozzarella on a giant pizza. Finally it was three thirty and I could barely keep my arms folded straight as Mrs Platini chose which table could be dismissed first.

Then Kiersten and I had to do Sainsbury's which I usually can't stand—especially the fruit and vegetable section which takes forever—but it wasn't that bad this time because I had fun choosing packed lunch things for Jolene and me to eat next week. 'Shall I get smoked turkey or salami? Or what if she's vegetarian? Is she a vegetarian?' I asked.

'I don't know.' Kiersten frowned. 'I shouldn't think so.'

'What about potato chips—I mean crisps? What do you reckon? Salt and vinegar? Prawn cocktail?'

'I don't know—get both.'

'You don't know? Kiersten, these are basics! My grandma Tor knows my favourite brands.'

'What's that supposed to mean?' Mom snapped. She glared at me for a second before pushing the trolley further down the aisle.

I stared after her, wondering where the attitude had come from. I hurried to catch up. 'Hey, I didn't mean anything. Don't get all humpy.'

Mom threw a tub of popcorn into the trolley. 'I'm not getting "humpy", Brody, but you need to get things straight. I do not figure in Jolene's life as anything other than the woman who is married to her grandad. She certainly doesn't see me as her grandma, any more than Claire sees me as her mom—it would be stupid, anyway, given the age gap, huh?'

'I guess so. I'm sorry.'

Kiersten saw the look on my face and chucked me under the chin. 'Don't look so miserable, honey. I just don't want you playing "happy families" when we're not.'

'What are we then? Unhappy families?'

'No! Just separate families—OK?'

'OK! I get your point. I only asked what kind of potato chips I should choose.'

Mom sighed and said cheese and onion, which was a weird suggestion as those were her least favourite.

Jake got back about six by which time Mom had made dinner and I had checked Jolene's bedroom was in order. We'd put her in the guest room, next to Mom and Dad's, with its high ceilings and awesome view out on to the orchard. I added a few special touches I thought she might appreciate—magazines and books, scented candles and tiny soaps. That kind of stuff. The room looked real homely by the time I had finished.

Downstairs, Jake was checking his watch. 'Has Claire phoned at all?' he asked as it got to seven thirty and there was still no sign of them.

'Not as far as I know,' Kiersten replied, loading the dishwasher noisily.

'I could have caught a later train,' Jake complained.

Boy, he was tetchy—just like Mom had been earlier. That's the trouble with having parents who run their own businesses. They can never switch off. Anything else is an inconvenience. I sometimes wonder what would happen if I didn't actually model for Dad and was just a plain old stay-at-home daughter. Would he even remember who I was?

'How were those shots of me on Jacob's Well Road?' I asked trying to distract him.

'Better than last time—we're still working on them,' Dad sniffed as he checked his mobile for messages.

'Enough "edge"?'

'Maybe,' he said vaguely.

Then again, maybe not, said the tone of his voice but I didn't have time to go into details because a few seconds later we heard the sound of a car on the gravel driveway. Mom slammed the door of the dishwasher and stared reproachfully at Jake, who just shrugged. Claire and Jolene had arrived.

Chapter Seven

The pair stood in the doorway, squinting under the brightness of the porch's nightlight. Jolene was standing slightly in front of Claire but stepped back as Jake approached. 'Come on in,' Jake greeted them, automatically going into enthusiastic-mode and holding the door open wide so they could enter.

'Hi!' I said, pushing forward, too impatient for all those stuffy English formalities. I went straight for Jolene and hugged her, ignoring what Mom had said in the supermarket earlier about not playing happy families. Jolene was family and I was happy to see her—simple.

My arms slid easily round Jolene's red and white striped football shirt. Wow, she was slender. She stiffened immediately, pulling back her head and shaking her long, fine blonde hair like a horse ready to bolt. 'It is so cool to have you here!' I gushed as Jake prised me off her.

'Let the poor girl breathe,' he rebuked.

The 'poor girl' stared at me through hostile greeny-blue eyes. I guess I had been a little over-the-top. 'Sorry,' I apologized, 'I've just been looking forward to your visit so much.'

Jolene didn't say a thing. She just turned towards Claire and glowered at her as if to say 'get me out of here'. I looked eagerly from my niece to my half-sister, expecting some kind of greeting, but her attention was fully focused on Jolene, whom she began to prod in the back with a sharp fingernail. 'Right, you, just remember what I've said, you behave yourself at your grandad's; I don't want any more of your nonsense. Understand?'

'Get lost,' Jolene mumbled angrily.

'You get lost!' Claire hissed back, before turning to Jake. 'Then she wonders why she's not going to Euro Disney with us!' she exclaimed.

'Ask me if I'm bothered?' Jolene retorted.

I glanced at Mom, who rolled her eyes heavenwards as if to say, 'I knew it would be like this.'

'OK, OK, let's go through into the front room and relax, huh?' Dad suggested, holding out his arm in a friendly gesture as Claire and Jolene continued to snipe at each other. Claire, who was tall and slim like Mom but with over-browned skin from what I guessed was too much time on sunbeds, broke off from her argument long enough to say she couldn't. 'No time; the flight's first thing in the morning and we've got to pack yet. Here's her stuff.' A red nylon backpack was hurriedly thrust into Jake's arms.

'Surely you'll stay for a coffee at least?' he asked nonplussed.

Claire glowered at her watch, as if to consider.

'Yeah, Mam. Stay,' Jolene said quietly and I knew that despite the argument, she didn't want her mom to leave.

'I can't,' Claire replied brusquely, again addressing Jake. 'Darryl's babysitting the lads and I promised I'd be back as soon as we could.'

'You always put them first, don't you?' Jolene muttered.

Claire retorted immediately. 'Well, whose fault's that? Maybe if you started behaving better like they do, I'd put you first.'

'Ask me if I'm bothered,' Jolene repeated but her voice wobbled as she said it.

'Hey, hey, Claire, come on, relax,' Dad said sharply.

I was glad he had interfered. The way Claire talked to Jolene made me feel uncomfortable. Claire's eyes narrowed as she turned on Jake. 'Relax? Huh! Chance would be a fine thing with this one.'

'Well, she can't be that bad. I don't see any ammo,' Dad said and winked at his granddaughter.

'That's right—undermine me like you always do,' Claire complained while Jolene fidgeted silently with the hem of her shirt. I decided I didn't like my half-sister Claire much. I mean, if I'd got this straight, the woman was dumping her daughter so she could take the rest of her family to Euro Disney. How unfair was that? Plus you could see she was itching to get away. She had barely stepped inside the hallway and even now was turning to check the car was still outside. Well, just go then, lady, I thought, and good riddance. I took Jolene by the elbow and pulled her closer to me. 'Jolene will be just fine with us, thanks, ma'am. You can leave now.'

Claire focused on me fully for the first time, running her eyes up and down me like a judge looking for faults in an exhibit. She seemed half-surprised, half-amused by me as I steadily returned her gaze. 'Ma'am? There's a new one! Get her to call me that instead of some of the stuff she comes out with and I'll give you a medal.' She shifted her gaze to the antiques in the hallway for a second before adding, 'Not that you need one.'

'Mam,' Jolene said, her voice wobbly, 'let me come back with you. I'll behave, honest.'

'No,' Claire said, shaking her head, 'it's too late for all that. You've made your bed—now you can lie in it.' Without another word, Claire turned and was gone.

Chapter Eight

None of us had expected Jolene to be left like that—so quickly and so coldly. We all stood around awkwardly in the hallway for a few seconds, then Mom and I broke out in conversation at once, both of us asking Jolene if she wanted to look at her room but our guest just stood rigidly by Dad's side, staring at the door. It was Jake who managed to coax her out of her trance. 'So, you're a Sunderland supporter?' he asked lightly.

Jolene half-nodded and I realized he was referring to the red and white shirt she was wearing. I'm not very up on soccer.

'I always followed the Toon myself, like,' Dad grinned.

I didn't have a clue what he was talking about but Jolene's jaw dropped open in horror. 'Newcastle? They're . . . ' and she used two of the foulest swear words possible to describe them.

Mom's eyes nearly shot out of her head but Dad roared with laughter. 'Well, it's an opinion!' he said, laying his hand lightly on his granddaughter's shoulder and leading her towards the warmth of the living room. 'So who's your favourite player, then?' he chatted on. I noticed Dad's Wearside accent became more and more broad as he talked, until there were 'hinnies' and 'wayayes' bouncing all over the joint. 'We could watch the pre-match reports on now, like,' he suggested, searching for the remote.

'Four-o-one,' Jolene mumbled, staring up at Dad as if she didn't quite believe him.

Dad punched in the number of this never-used channel and patted the couch beside him.

'Canny. Come and sit here then, Pet' Jake said, 'you'll get a better view.'

Cautiously, Jolene sat down, and for the next few hours her eyes never left the screen. I had the feeling she wasn't that interested in the commentary—I think it just gave her something familiar to do. She'd reply to Dad's questions warily but the several times I tried to start conversations up she ignored me completely, apart from darting me sidelong glances now and again. Dad peered over at me resignedly as if to show me he was bored too but eventually I got fed up with being blanked and I went to find Mom. Unfortunately, she was on the phone—fussing with Sarah Riley over the exhibition—so all I got from her was an apologetic smile.

That kind of set the whole pattern for the weekend. Jolene watched TV, barely spoke unless she was spoken to, and hardly acknowledged my presence at all. Dad said it was because she was shy and felt uncomfortable; Mum just sighed and said, 'What can you expect?' They had both been really kind to Jolene, despite their attitude in Piccollino's, and were bending over backwards to make her feel at home. She was even allowed Coke, because she told Dad that's all she drank.

By Sunday afternoon I was really frustrated. I'm an active kind of person and like doing things rather than watching other people do them on screen. Dad was in his study preparing for work on Monday and Mom was over at her kilns in the stable block. 'Do you want to explore outside in the orchard?' I asked Jolene. 'It's great for hide and seek and I think there are foxes living at the bottom.'

'No thanks,' she muttered, watching the credits roll by on the end of yet another cartoon.

'How about a swim in the pool?' I asked.

'Not brought me cossie.'

'I can lend you one.'

'No thanks—don't like swimming much.' She darted me one of her classic sidelong glances.

I sighed heavily and sat down on the arm of the chair near her. 'What would you like to do, then? I'll join in with anything you want.'

The girl hunched her shoulders and shrank into the couch. Anyone would think I had asked her to go sword swallowing or something. 'I want to stay here,' she said and reached out for her glass of Coke. She was about to take a drink when an advert for Euro Disney came on the screen. Her face clouded over and her mouth wobbled slightly as Mickey and Goofy waved their giant rubbery hands at us.

'I bet it's not that great,' I said, trying to make her feel better. 'I heard you have to queue for hours to get on the rides—especially Space Mountain.'

'I suppose,' she said miserably.

I tried to think of something that would cheer her. 'After School club's neat,' I said, 'we're doing film-making.' Even to me it sounded a bit lame compared to Space Mountain.

But Jolene wasn't interested. Her face hardened. 'I hope the car crashes,' she hissed, staring at the TV screen. 'I hope it crashes and Darryl and Keith and Jack get killed so I can have me mam all to myself for once.'

'Oh,' I said shocked, 'that's kind of harsh!'

'I don't care,' she declared, 'it'd be great.'

'I thought they were going by plane?' I said.

Jolene stared stonily at the screen. 'Whatever.'

She reached calmly across for more Coke and I figured a change of subject might not be a bad idea. I glanced towards the door, then took a chance. 'Jolene, do you mind if I have a taste of that?' I asked.

'If you want,' she said, and handed me her glass.

I whispered conspiratorially to her. 'I'm not

allowed it usually. Jake reckons my teeth will drop out,' and I put the glass to my lips. Just as the first drops of the delicious liquid touched my tongue I heard a door open in the outer hallway and panicked. 'Take it back, quick!' I ordered but Jolene had moved and I watched helplessly as the glass slid from my hand and into her lap, splashing Coke everywhere. She leapt up with a yell and the glass smashed onto the wooden floor.

'My shirt!' she shouted angrily, as Coke dripped down it like dark rain. 'Look at my shirt!' For once there were no sidelong glances. Her angry eyes were trained fully on me but I was too busy trying not to tread on broken glass and too worried about what Dad would say to feel the full force of her stare.

'Sorry,' I yelled, 'sorry, sorry.'

Of course, Dad rushed in, wondering what all the racket was about. He grabbed a handful of paper tissues from a nearby box and started to gather the shards in them. 'Oh, Brody, you know you need to be more careful with glass. What happened?'

'She's knacked my shirt, that's what happened,' Jolene stated bitterly before I could explain.

Jake glanced at it and told her it would wash. 'And steady with the language,' he added.

'What am I supposed to wear on top, then? A carrier bag?' Jolene demanded rudely.

I would never have dared talk to Jake like that but Jolene seemed not to care. I guessed it was what she was used to with Claire.

'Just put something else on,' Jake replied.

'Like what?' she snapped, rubbing furiously at the stain.

'Well, I suggest you change into a T-shirt or a jumper. I also suggest you change your attitude while you're at it,' Dad said, trying to sound calm but there was a tiny pulse in his neck that always shows when he's angry or irritated and it was beating rapidly.

Jolene opened her mouth to speak, glanced at me, then Jake, and thought better of it.

'Sorry,' she mumbled, 'it's just I didn't bring anything else. I only pretended to pack when Mam told me, I . . . I hadn't planned on stopping here, had I?'

'That's OK,' Jake said, more gently, 'Brody will lend you something.'

I apologized again for spilling Coke on Jolene's shirt as we headed to my bedroom. 'Yeah, well, accidents happen,' Jolene mumbled, 'though I don't know why you had to go so divvy in front of Grandad. It's only a bloomin' drink.' She gave me one of her looks but I knew there was no point explaining about how I have to take care of myself at all times. It was a model-thing and she wouldn't understand.

I tried to be cheerful. 'Anyway, this'll be fun. You can choose anything you want from my closets. I'll do your hair, too—maybe try out a few styles? It's so straight—I wish mine was straight—you can do so much more with it.'

Jolene frowned heavily. I guessed make-overs might not be her thing.

I led her into my bedroom and opened my closets. I have a whole row stretching across one wall, all arranged according to the seasons, but as I flung one outfit after another on to my bed, Jolene just pulled

46

one sour face after another. 'Nah—too cissy, nah—too poncy,' she said. Boy, was she fussy for someone with only one shirt to wear. She wasn't even impressed by the Funky Punk outfit when I showed it to her. 'I'm just not girly,' she said flatly, 'and that's that.'

Eventually she chose a baggy old *Lakers* sweatshirt. 'This'll do,' she sniffed, leaving before I even had a chance to style her hair. I stared after her and sighed. This *so* wasn't how I had imagined the weekend would turn out.

Chapter Nine

I spent the rest of the evening in my room. I had tried
again with Jolene later on but she had reverted to the
eyes-glued-to-the-TV-set routine and there was no
way I could face that again. Besides, I had homework
to finish—a couple of projects for Mrs Platini and
some vocabulary work for Mrs Morgan. Mom
appeared at some stage and made supper and then
took Jolene off to show her where to wash her shirt—
Jolene didn't trust Mom to do it for her. I was heading
back upstairs when Jake called me through into his
study.

'I just wanted a quiet word,' he said, closing the
door behind us.

'Hush,' I said.

'What?'

'That's a quiet word.'

He looked puzzled. 'Joke, Jake,' I explained.

His face cleared. 'Oh, right. Sorry, Brody, I'm a bit distracted.' He began packing his holdall, throwing his Filofax randomly on top of files and assorted padded envelopes.

'What gives, Jake?' I asked.

'It's about Jolene. I want you to look after her at this After School club thing this week.'

'Well, duh! What did you think I was going to do?' I asked.

He looked at me gravely. 'Hey, don't you start with the sarcasm—I need you to take this seriously. I do not have family crisis on my schedule for this week. If I don't nail this Funky Punk thing soon I'm going to be in a mess—I'm way behind as it is.'

'Oh,' I said, 'that serious.'

'Yes, that serious, so keep Jolene away from trouble, right?'

'Why would she even get into trouble?' I asked.

Dad scratched the back of his neck. 'Because she's on a short fuse, just like her mother always was—or still is. All the same signs are there.'

'You mean like with the Coke thing?'

'Yes, I mean the Coke thing and the answering back thing and the bad language thing. Claire was just the same—fine as long as she got her own way, foul if she didn't; and then, of course, it's everybody else's fault. I have no time for it—no time at all.'

'Jolene's not that bad, is she?' I said.

Dad sighed. 'I'm not saying she is, but Jolene's obviously no angel or she wouldn't be here. That gets me as well—being used like that. Claire needs to get her act together . . . and fast. Anyway, I'm just relying on you to look after Jolene. Don't let me down—I'm relying on you, Brody.'

'I won't let you down, I promise,' I told him.

'I know you won't,' he said, smiling. 'You're the daughter I got right.'

Chapter Ten

My promise to watch over Jolene was the first thing I thought of when I woke up the next morning. Not because of Dad's fear of trouble, but because she looked so edgy when she realized he had gone. 'He didn't say goodbye,' she said.

'He never does,' I explained, 'he leaves too early. Didn't he tell you last night?'

'Maybe. I can't remember.'

'He'll be back Wednesday,' Kiersten added. Jolene just shrugged, looking distrustfully from one to the other of us as if wondering who was going to pounce on her first.

'Can I make you some raisin toast?' I asked.

'If you want,' she replied dully.

'Butter?'

'Not bothered,' she mumbled.

'What would you like in your packed lunch?'

'Not bothered.'

Not bothered and a few shrugs were the best I could get out of her over breakfast but I guess some people are just not morning folk. I hoped she'd perk up once we got to After School club.

Mom dropped us off and I led Jolene into the playground. Being vacation time, the place was deserted and it was a bit spooky without everyone milling around but I knew once we were inside the mobile it would be more lively. I hoped so, anyway; I wanted Jolene to get some kind of buzz from being here.

'It'll be neat,' I reassured her, 'really.' I began filling her in with details about the film-making activity and Mrs Fryston and how cool everyone was. Just ahead, I could see Sammie waiting. 'That's Sammie—she's nice but she's got a thing about waiting there for me every day for some reason,' I whispered.

We reached the mobile steps and Sammie immediately moved aside to let us through, giving

Jolene an inquisitive stare as she did so. 'Hi, Sammie,' I said and introduced her to Jolene.

They appraised each other carefully. 'Hello,' Sammie greeted her, finally smiling broadly.

Jolene muttered something in reply that could have been a hello.

'Is Mrs Fryston here yet?' I asked Sammie.

'Yes.'

'Oh, OK, see you inside then?'

'Brody?'

'Aha?'

'Did you find our Gemma's headband yet?'

My hand shot to my mouth. 'I forgot all about it—I'm sorry, Sammie—tomorrow?'

'All right,' she said dully, glancing at Jolene who had let out an enormous yawn.

Jolene kept her head bent all the time I introduced her to the others. I guessed it was pretty hard for her,

being surrounded by new people, but she could at least have said hello. All she did was stare at the floor. Reggie, Lloyd, Sam, and even Brandon drifted away when they couldn't get a response from her.

I glanced around, wondering what I could do that might grab her attention. The guys running the film-making course, students from Bretton College, weren't due to arrive until ten thirty so Mrs Fryston had told us we could either play a game or make a photograph frame with Mrs McCormack on the craft table. I asked Jolene what she wanted to do. 'Not bothered,' she shrugged.

'How about Jenga? Or Battleships? Kerplunk?'

'I don't mind making a frame,' she whispered.

'OK.'

We sat opposite Alex and another girl. I tried again. 'Hi, everyone—this is my cousin Jolene,' I said. I knew she wasn't technically my cousin but Mom thought it would be easier to explain.

I don't think Alex was going to bother replying, what with Jolene being with me and all, until she saw Jolene's top. 'That's a Sunderland shirt, isn't it?' she asked.

'Yeah,' Jolene replied slowly and I thought to myself, not stupid soccer *again*.

'My next-door neighbour supports them. She travels everywhere to see them,' Alex informed my niece.

'Does she?' Jolene said, bucking up a little.

'Yes. She even painted the front of her house in red and white stripes once and she's called it "Stadium of Light" instead of "Prospect Place". Mum complained to the council, didn't you? So she had to paint over it.'

Mrs McCormack nodded. 'I certainly did! Smack bang in the middle of an Edwardian terrace? It stuck out like a sore thumb.'

'I think that was the whole idea, Mum,' Alex said, rolling her eyes at Jolene.

Jolene rolled hers back and something clicked between them. I felt it. Alex slid a cardboard template over to Jolene and silently passed her a saucer full of beads which had been half-hidden beneath her jumper. Jolene reached for the glue and that was that.

Over the next half-hour they seemed to do the same thing simultaneously. Alex chose blue beads for her frame; Jolene chose blue beads for her frame. Jolene opted for gold glitter round the blue beads—Alex opted for silver. Neither paid much attention to what they were actually doing—they were too engrossed in their conversation for that. Mrs McCormack raised her eyebrows at me and smiled as if to say, 'Isn't that nice?'

Forget it, lady, I thought. There was no way that relationship was going anywhere but nowhere. Dad instructed me to keep Jolene out of trouble, not leap straight into it.

When Mrs Fryston clapped her hands together for our attention and told us the students had arrived, I pulled Jolene away. 'Let's go over here,' I said and had her follow me across to Reggie.

Chapter Eleven

The three students Mrs Fryston introduced us to were called Sunreep, Will, and Denise. I liked the look of Denise immediately. She was black with the most fantastic coloured weaves in her hair that reached right down to the middle of her back. Her smile took in the whole room and I had a sudden pang of homesickness for my grade four teacher back in the States.

Will took the lead. 'OK, kids, let's see how quickly you can get into three groups.'

Jolene and I were already sitting with Reggie, Lloyd, and Brandon so I didn't have any problem telling Alex we had enough people in our group when she approached.

'One more won't hurt,' she said and plonked herself straight down on the other side of Jolene. Jolene smiled at her and shuffled up. I could see I was going to have to warn her away from Alex as soon as I got the chance.

'OK.' Will smiled, rubbing his hands together. 'Right then, let's get some action going. Who likes films like James Bond with all the car chases and special effects? Or things like *X-Men* where the characters have super-powers like morphing into another shape?'

Several hands shot up. 'OK, well, forget all that!' he said and he grinned at Mrs Fryston as everyone groaned with disappointment, just as he had expected they would. 'We're going to keep things nice and simple. This is the idea: each group will make a short film based around a traditional fairytale—you know, like "Cinderella" or "Snow White" or *Scream 2*. Each member of the group will take part by acting in it as well as dealing with the technical side, so you're all going to be very busy but the end result will be that everyone will have a video to take home. We might even have time for a film show on Friday afternoon. Bring your own popcorn.'

'This is dead smart,' Reggie whispered to me. 'I'm going to be a film producer when I grow up and I'm already getting work experience. Just think, Miller, you'll be able to tell people you knew me at school.'

I dug him in the ribs, first because I hate it when he calls me Miller, and second because Denise was heading straight towards us.

'Hello,' she said, a friendly smile on her face, 'shall we go find a space and get started?'

Our group decided we'd tackle 'Little Red Riding Hood' except it would be called 'Little Reggie Riding Hood'. There's a clue in the title as to who played the main part. I got to be the wolf, Brandon the woodcutter, Jolene surprisingly agreed to be the granny, and then a few fabricated roles were thrown in—Lloyd was Mr Hood, Reggie's dad, and Alex was Mrs Hood, Reggie's mom. The idea was to design the scenes so whoever wasn't acting would be filming.

Everyone seemed absorbed by the project from the start. Lloyd kept coming out with neat ideas about props and scenery and I was real surprised when Alex and Jolene added their suggestions, too. I began to relax. So far so good.

Reggie then suggested we begin working in pairs on the scripts. 'Shall we go over there and write a scene together?' I suggested to Jolene.

'I suppose,' she muttered, glancing at Alex.

'Can't we work in a three?' Alex wanted to know.

'Not really,' I replied instantly.

I didn't see Reggie hovering nearby. 'Er . . . person in need of a partner here,' he announced, looking straight at me.

Alex's face lit up. 'You go with him and I'll go with Jolene,' she decided and before I had a chance to say anything she linked arms with my niece and my usually don't-touch-me niece linked back as if she'd been best buddies with Alex for years. I couldn't help feeling a little sore. I mean, I'd bent over backwards all weekend to bond with Jolene and got nowhere, but two minutes with the book pincher and she's Miss Congeniality.

Reggie doled out the tasks. Boy, he was so motivated. He kept pushing his glasses up the bridge of his nose and spouting out orders. No one seemed to mind—it was Reggie, after all. He never said anything in a bossy way and it did save a lot of hassle having someone take charge. Within minutes the next Steven Spielberg had drawn up a plan of action on a sheet of sugar paper. He had Alex and Jolene work on the opening scene: 'At home with the Hoods, somewhere near the woods'; Brandon worked with Lloyd using Denise as secretary to help Brandon with the writing, on scene two: 'Wolf has lunch—Special of the Day: Raw Granny'. And finally he announced our scene was to be: 'What big eyes you've got for someone with cataracts'.

'We'll write ours in Yorkshire, Miller,' Reggie decided. 'It can get nominated for best foreign language film then. How does this sound? "Reggie Ridin' 'Ud: What great big eyes tha's got, our gran. Wolf: All the better for seeing thi' with, pet lamb".'

'Pet lamb's good,' I said. 'A hint at the character's true eating habits.'

'Course it's good—I'm a genius,' Reggie declared matter-of-factly and he began scribbling away.

Chapter Twelve

'This is the best time I've ever spent in a school,' Jolene declared as Kiersten picked us up that night. 'Except for when I set the fire alarm off during the road safety quiz.'

'Glad to hear it,' Mom grinned, smiling at me as if to say, 'Isn't that nice, apart from the fire alarm thing.'

'Do you know Alex McCormack, Mrs McCormack's daughter?' Jolene asked Kiersten chattily. It was the most animated I'd seen her round Mom since she arrived.

'Yes, I think so—by sight anyway,' Mom said.

'She's my best friend,' Jolene declared, a huge beam on her face.

'Oh, that's sweet—maybe she could come to tea before you go back home,' Mom replied.

My heart thumped painfully in my chest. 'Don't

make any definite arrangements,' I interrupted, before Jolene had time to start ordering in pizza, 'you know how unpredictable this week is for you. It would be dumb if you fixed up something then had to cancel.'

'That's true,' Kiersten agreed. 'Maybe another time, Jolene.'

Jolene scowled at me but I didn't care. There was no way Alex was coming to my house. Not for all the doughnuts in Denver.

Film-making Day Two was polishing the scripts, and adding helpful directions in the margins of the storyboard like: 'side shot of bed', 'close up of "granny's" neck being chopped— NB: use cardboard axe, not real one'. Then Denise had us all handling the video cameras. I tried hard to listen when it was my turn to learn but it was difficult to do that and keep an eye on Jolene at the same time.

She was settling in fast. The girl who had entered the mobile yesterday with her eyes drilling holes in the carpet was now laughing out loud at something Alex had said, making everyone stop and stare. I sighed, thinking how much easier my job would have been if Jolene had stuck with me. I was going to have to do something before it all got too silly. What, I didn't know.

Reggie brought me out of my stupor by rapping his knuckles on my skull. 'Hello! Anyone home?' he shouted in my ear.

'What? Oh, sorry, got other things on my mind,' I said as we made way for Brandon and Lloyd on the camera and returned to our storyboard.

'Focus, Miller—I can't do all of it, I need your help,' Reggie told me peevishly.

'Glad someone does,' I mumbled, glancing down at Jolene as we passed. She didn't even notice.

'She's not going to get lost, you know,' Reggie said.

'Who?'

'Her—that cousin of yours. You follow her round like a lemon.'

'You don't understand,' I told him.

'You're right, I don't,' he agreed. 'But I know one thing, you've turned into a right miserable mare since she came.'

'Thank you so much,' I grunted.

He pushed his glasses higher up the bridge of his nose. 'You're welcome,' he said.

Chapter Thirteen

Wednesday morning, Day Three, was the read-through for each scene so we could start thinking about stage directions and positioning of actors and cameras for when we started filming in the afternoon. The whole project was hotting up and there was a real buzz in every corner of the After School club. For my part, I had decided Reggie was right—I had turned into a 'miserable mare' this week, so I was trying to make it up to him by collaborating harder on his script. Alex and Jolene were fully occupied practising with the video camera, so I was free to work on my Yorkshire accent, which Reggie thought was 'right pathetic'.

'OK,' Reggie began, 'you're under the duvet and I come in. I put your shopping on the foot of the bed . . .'

'Are you sure Granny would have ordered lager and pork pies? It doesn't seem appropriate somehow,' I interrupted.

Reggie pursed his lips. 'It's called improvisation, Brody, and every actor worth their salt does it. Anyway, my gran lives on Baileys and Cornish pasties so I don't see why this one can't live on lager and pork pies. Now, can we get started?'

'Yes, sir.'

Reggie cleared his throat. 'My, what big eyes tha's got, our gran,' he boomed, zooming in close and staring into my eyes.

'All the better to see thi' wi', Reggie Riding Hood,' I said, stumbling across each word.

''Ud,' Reggie corrected, ''Ud.'

''Ud.'

'You've got nice eyes by the way,' he mumbled.

'Shut up,' I mumbled back.

The actor-director cleared his throat once more. 'My, what great big lug 'oles tha's got, our gran,' he boomed again, zooming in so close to my ear he filled it with his warm breath.

'All the better to hear you with, Reggie Riding 'Ud,' I said, trying not to giggle because it tickled.

' 'Ear you with,' Reggie corrected, ' 'ear.'

I threw down my script in exasperation. 'What exactly is your gripe with the eighth letter of the alphabet in this county?'

'I don't know—just get on with it, woman,' he replied and punched me lightly on the arm.

I punched him back. 'Don't start summat you can't finish!' I warned him.

He laughed and shouted across to the rest of our group. 'Summat? Eh—Lloydy—did you hear that? Miller over here said "summat". We'll turn her into a northerner yet!'

At break I walked over to the craft table to give Jolene her snack but she waved it away. 'It's all right—Alex already gave me this.' She showed me a half-eaten bar of sticky pink and white nougat. It looked gross and I felt rejected again, thinking of all that time I'd spent choosing things for her in Sainsbury's last week.

'Oh. Well, don't just fill up on junk, will you? We're having a meal in Piccollino's tonight with Jake, remember,' I said. He was coming home for his mid-week stop-over.

Jolene shrugged. 'That's ages away,' she pointed out before casually informing me that Alex reckoned Reggie fancied me. 'She says it's dead obvious.'

I got kind of defensive—I don't know why. It hadn't exactly been a secret I had liked Reggie once but I just didn't like being teased about it by Alex. 'He does not! Alex talks out of her butt,' I replied without thinking.

Jolene's face clouded over slightly but she carried on eating the gluey nougat, her eyes fixed on mine. She ate rapidly, gnawing it like a squirrel until finally tossing the remaining stump in the direction of the waste basket. It missed. 'Aren't you going to pick that up?' I asked, as Mrs Fryston looked across inquisitively.

'Nah, I'll let you,' Jolene said breezily and she walked away. My, she sure was feeling at home.

It was lunchtime when the whole thing went pear-shaped. I was eating my packed lunch with half the cast of *Reggie Riding Hood*, a quarter of the cast of *Snow Bite* (the vampire version), and all of *Pop Idols* (Sammie's group not quite getting to grips with the idea of traditional stories), when Brandon arrived, trying not to cry but not quite managing to stop the tears. 'Brody,' he sniffed, tugging at me, 'they've taken "Peas" again.'

'Who have?'

'Alex and that other girl. They've hidded it and they're laughing at me.'

My heart sank. I really didn't want to have to deal with this.

'Can't you tell Mrs Fryston? Or Denise?'

'I don't know where they is,' Brandon said, his chest heaving up and down. That book meant so much to him.

I twisted round. Sure enough, Alex had *Eat Your Peas* tucked under her arm and was heading for the cloakroom with it.

'Wait here, guy, I won't be long,' I told him.

'Thank you, Brody,' he sniffed. 'You're my hero.'

Chapter Fourteen

When I couldn't find them in the cloakroom or any of the toilet cubicles, I realized the pair had gone outside, even though it was drizzling heavily, and out of bounds. Jolene and Alex were standing outside the mobile, on the small platform leading down the steps, eating chocolate. Alex was spouting forth in a forced whisper anyone passing within fifty metres could overhear. '. . . And Mr Sharkey, who's our head teacher, right, he's going out with Mrs Fryston but they're keeping it quiet because his divorce has only just come through and it might look bad.'

Where had that juicy bit of information come from, McCormack? I wondered. Jolene nodded interestedly as Alex continued gossiping for Great Britain. 'Mrs

Fryston's told my mum she's having trouble with her two teenage daughters about it because they don't like her having a boyfriend.'

'Huh! Tell me about it!' Jolene said.

'She's never had one since her husband died, you see.'

My, she knew her stuff. Across the playing field, I could see Mr Sharkey, who had obviously forgotten he should have been on vacation, talking to the caretaker. I thought it might be a good idea to stop any further revelations in case the Head decided to 'drop in' on the Nut in the Hut sometime soon. 'Hi, you guys,' I said, stepping round the door to join them, trying to keep it light. 'How you doing?'

Their gaze told me they weren't overjoyed to see me, so I got straight to the point. 'Erm . . . is it OK if I have that book for Brandon? You know what he's like about it,' I said, addressing Alex.

She pulled it closer to her. 'No. We want it for a prop in the play. It's Mrs Hood's newspaper.'

'Couldn't you use another book instead?' I asked.

Jolene shrugged and I could tell it wouldn't have mattered either way to her but Alex pursed her lips and scowled. 'No,' she repeated, 'why should I? It's not his, like I told you last time.'

Yeah, I thought, I remember. 'Oh, chill out, Alex, it's no skin off your nose which book you use, is it?' I said. 'He's only a little boy.'

Her face paled, as if I'd said something outrageous. 'So what? Why should they get their own way all the time? It's not fair.'

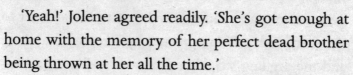

'Yeah!' Jolene agreed readily. 'She's got enough at home with the memory of her perfect dead brother being thrown at her all the time.'

'That was a secret,' Alex muttered to Jolene.

'Sorry, Alex,' Jolene replied instantly.

I tried again. 'Come on, Alex, just give me the book and I'll bring you another one, huh?'

Alex squared her shoulders and pushed the book out of reach. 'Get lost, Brody Miller. You think you rule, don't you, just because you're a model. Well, you don't!'

Where had that come from? 'I so do not think that! Get a life, Alex,' I said, becoming irritated. I turned to

Jolene. 'I wouldn't hang out with her so much if I were you—she's too immature for you.'

It was so the wrong thing to say. Jolene's eyes narrowed and her face tightened as it had when I'd spilt her Coke that time. 'I'll hang out with who I like so don't call my friends names or else,' she threatened.

Alex giggled and I felt myself blushing hard but I bit back my reply. I did not want to enter into the whole answering back deal I knew Jolene was so good at. The last thing I needed was Dad arriving at the station and getting at me for causing a commotion. Mom, too, for that matter. She was still chasing those dumb perspex units and had to travel over to Manchester to get them today. Being greeted by a report on Jolene and me arguing wouldn't go down well after a long journey in the rain. Sorry, Brandon, I thought, I can't be your hero today. 'OK, OK,' I said to Jolene, 'it's nothing to get worked up about. I'm out of here.'

I began to retreat but Jolene hadn't finished. I noticed her breathing had changed; it was now coming out in strange, rapid breaths, as if she had been exercising heavily. Distracted, I didn't see the finger which darted towards me suddenly and poked me so hard in the chest, my head bounced against the door. Alex stared too, seeming as startled as I was. 'Alex is right,' Jolene continued heatedly, 'you do think you rule and that you can boss people round all the time, don't you? You even bossed my mum around!'

'When?' I said, rubbing my head.

'When we arrived. You almost shoved her out of the house like you were the queen or something.'

'I was just trying to help you,' I said quietly, 'she was being mean to you.'

My niece focused on me once again, pushing her face closer and closer to mine so I could smell chocolate on her breath. 'My mam's not mean! She'd have taken me with her if you hadn't stuck your oar in!'

'I don't think she would—she said you'd made your bed and you had to lie in it,' I pointed out.

'Shut up, you!' Jolene roared, tears gathering in her dark eyes. 'Shut up! Shut up! You don't know anything about her. She was only trying to teach me a lesson. She would never have left me if you hadn't interfered and that's a fact, that is.'

'I didn't get that impression,' I said in a small voice.

But Jolene hadn't finished. 'Oh, you want an impression? I'll give you an impression. Who's this? "Yes, Daddy, no, Daddy, course I won't drink Coke, Daddy." You're feeble, you are. You're just a big feeble creep, like Jack and Keith. A big, stupid goody-two-shoes feeble creep who does everything you're told cos you haven't got a brain of your own!' She sprang back, stepping agitatedly from side to side, clenching and unclenching her fists, eyes trained on me, full beam and frightening.

I glanced at Alex, thinking she'd be enjoying the spectacle, but to my surprise she looked as afraid and bewildered as I felt. 'What's up? Cat got your tongue?' Jolene goaded me. 'That's a first, isn't it? Yap, yap, yap—that's all you do—talk. It does my head in! Go on, say something now!'

Say something so I've got an excuse to whack you is what she meant. I just stared at her blankly. I had never been in a fight situation before and my brain seemed to have seized up. I stood there mutely, just waiting. 'Go on!' Jolene repeated, coiled and dangerous. 'Say something!'

'She doesn't need to say nothing to you!' a familiar

voice shouted from behind me. Jolene stopped pacing for a split second as Sammie announced herself by banging the door behind her and glaring at Jolene through her orange fringe.

'Go away you!' Jolene barked at her. 'This is private.'

'Go away yourself!' Sammie barked back, standing squarely in-between Jolene and me. I had hardly seen Sammie all week—she had not even been on the steps to greet me the last two mornings—but I had been so preoccupied with Jolene and Alex, it hadn't registered. She was here now though, as solid as a stone wall. It was somehow reassuring. I cautiously edged round to give myself a little more space on the crowded platform. The drizzle had turned to rain as if to dramatize the whole sorry scene. 'Back off!' Sammie ordered. 'You can't talk to Brody like that, even if you are related! An' if anyone's feeble round here, it's you!'

'Says you and whose army?' Jolene sneered.

Alex opened her mouth to speak but closed it again. 'Why don't you go get . . .' I began, thinking this might be a good time to find an adult. Mr Sharkey, preferably, but he seemed to have disappeared from view.

'No,' Jolene shouted shrilly, misinterpreting what I had meant, '*you* get lost!'

'I wasn't going to say that!' I protested but she

wasn't listening. Whatever rage she had been suppressing finally erupted. Arms outstretched, Jolene lunged forward and pushed hard, sending Sammie careering helplessly into me. I automatically reached behind to hold on to the wooden rail as Sammie struggled to stay upright but I slipped on the wet floorboards and missed it. Sammie went one way and I went the other, toppling down the steps and onto the gravel border beside the mobile, face first.

A burning sensation seared across my mouth but it didn't really register. I heard someone scream, then I was dimly aware of Denise holding a huge towel over

my mouth and telling me to keep calm, keep calm, as she guided me to Mrs Fryston who was waiting by her open car. I think Mr Sharkey appeared at some point, ushering everyone back into the mobile, but I was already being driven away by then.

Chapter Fifteen

Mrs Fryston slid her mobile phone into her bag once more as we waited for an emergency appointment with Dr Willows, my dentist, having been directed straight there after seeing a doctor in the same medical centre complex. 'I've tried all your contact numbers but nobody's answering,' Mrs Fryston informed me worriedly. 'I'll keep trying, though. Is your mum out today?'

From somewhere in my cotton-wool brain, I registered I needed to nod.

'I expect she's at the exhibition, is she? It's very good,' Mrs Fryston told me, 'I went on Saturday with—I went on Saturday. I really liked the bowls with the seahorse design . . .' Mrs Fryston chatted nervously but I wasn't really taking any of it in and I don't think she expected me to. I felt shaky and numb and sick.

Eventually, the dental nurse called me through. 'Do you want me to come, too?' Mrs Fryston asked me. I nodded again. I needed someone familiar with me.

In the surgery, I slid reluctantly onto the black leather chair and felt even more sick and shaky as Dr Willows operated the lever to make the chair recline.

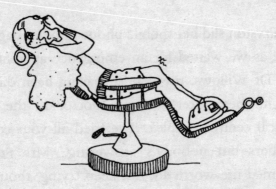

'Let's see what we've got here, shall we?' Dr Willows asked, moving her gloved hand to take the towel away. I clung to it at first, then began crying quietly as she gently coaxed it out of my grip. I already knew what she was going to find. I had run the tip of my tongue over the gap where my front tooth used to be.

The dentist grimaced when she saw. 'Oh dear, what a shame.'

'What is it?' Mrs Fryston asked huskily from her chair behind me.

She gave it to her straight. 'Her upper left incisor is broken right off, almost to the gum.' I winced and poor Mrs Fryston let out a gasp.

'Did you have the other bit of tooth with you?' Dr Willows asked.

I couldn't see but sensed Mrs Fryston shaking her head. 'I never thought to look—I just wanted to get her here as fast as possible,' she apologized.

'I doubt we could have glued it back anyway.' Dr Willows sighed. 'The tooth's broken too near to the gum, though I should be able to use the part that's left to build up a temporary new tooth to protect the damaged area until we get a veneer made. I'll have to take the nerve out, I'm afraid.' She looked at me kindly. 'It'll mean an injection, Brody, to stop you feeling any pain.'

The dentist then turned to her assistant and gave instructions. I squeezed my eyes shut and didn't look as the cold needle was slowly inserted into my gum. I tried to be brave. I tried counting to ten and thinking positive thoughts but I couldn't. I just cried noiseless,

salty tears because I knew nobody would be saying,
'Show me your beautiful smile', ever again.

Chapter Sixteen

When Dr Willows had patched me up the best she could and made me a fresh appointment for the next stage of treatment, Mrs Fryston led me back to the car. 'What do you want me to do?' she asked. 'I could drive round to the gallery and see if your mum's there, or take you back to school?'

'Mom's in Manchester,' I managed to reveal at last, my words crawling sluggishly over my thick tongue. I glanced at my reflection in the side mirror. As well as having a new fake tooth that felt like someone had stuck a house brick in there, one side of my face was scratched and grazed from where I'd ploughed into the gravel. My hands and knees, too, were gritty and sore. The girl from the States was in a state.

'Ah,' Mrs Fryston sighed, clicking in her seatbelt. 'Back to Zetland Avenue then.'

She drove slowly, even though there wasn't a lot of traffic around. 'Well, what a palaver, hm?' she mused. 'Can you remember what happened, Brody? I'll have to write out an accident form, you see. It's best to do it as soon as possible.'

I stared out of the window. The rain had stopped and everything was a washed-out dull grey. What had happened? I'd messed up, that's what had happened. Dad had asked me to keep Jolene out of trouble and I'd let him down, totally. Boy, was he going to be unhappy tonight. The thought of his reaction worried me more than any missing tooth.

I knew I was being dumb—I was the injured party here, right? But Jolene got it in one when she'd mocked me for being a—what was it?—a feeble, goody-two-shoes. When it came to my dad, I admit it, I didn't like letting him down. I would do anything to please him, from skipping school to avoiding cola. No way would I ever back-chat him the way she back-chatted her mom. Why? Because I was such a suck-up? Nope. Because I knew where I stood in the scheme of things. Jake Miller was no family guy. He put photography first, Kiersten second, and me third.

I didn't mind—it was just the way it was with a lot of creative types. But I didn't want to drop any further in the chart. Didn't want to end up like Claire, discarded like Sammie's headband because she wasn't to his liking. I mean, she was his first daughter and he hardly saw her, and Jolene was his only granddaughter and neither he nor Mom even knew what her favourite potato chips were. Call me whatever you wanted but I liked being the daughter he got right. It was a secure place to be.

But I'd messed up and he was going to be so cheesed off when he came back unless . . . my brain began spinning ideas together . . . unless I could persuade everyone it was just an accident. I mean, I fell, right? And if it hadn't been wet . . . and if Sammie hadn't fallen into me . . . 'I slipped,' I said finally to Mrs Fryston. 'We were just talking outside and I slipped.'

When we got to the main school building, Mrs Fryston nodded towards the reception area. 'Looks like Mr Sharkey's got everyone in there,' she said. 'Shall we go and get an update?'

I shrugged. Might as well face my demons one at a time, starting with Jolene. 'It all sounds very quiet,'

Mrs Fryston said to me, and she knocked on the office door.

I straightened my shoulders and walked in. I pretended I was modelling, focusing only on getting to the end of the catwalk and back. 'Hi,' I said, addressing no one in particular, 'what's new?'

Mr Sharkey, Alex, Sammie, and Jolene were all crammed together, competing with filing cabinets and computer desks and a mini pool-table for space. Everyone turned to stare as we entered. I made myself look directly at Jolene, to check out if she'd left Lake Psycho and calmed down. Her eyes met mine sullenly before she glanced away.

Mr Sharkey spoke first. 'Oh, dear, Brody, you have been in the wars, haven't you? Sit down, flower.'

Sammie was out of her seat like a shot. 'Sit here, Brody,' she said, her eyes filling with tears for some reason. I really wasn't hurt *that* much—no broken bones or anything. As I sat in her place she dragged a well-used tissue from her cardigan sleeve and blew hard.

'We're just trying to sort things out,' Mr Sharkey said, 'but we're not getting very far. Everyone seems to have taken a vow of silence—most peculiar.'

Everything did remain unbearably quiet for a few more seconds, then Alex spoke. She was sitting in the furthest corner, her head and shoulders partially obscured by a netball trophy. 'I'm really sorry, Brody,' she said timidly.

I looked at her in surprise.

'I'm really sorry—about what happened . . . outside.' She glanced from me to Jolene then back again. I remembered how distressed she had been when Jolene had lost her temper. She still seemed quite shaken.

'It's OK,' I mumbled.

'And I'm sorry for always teasing Brandon . . . you know . . . over the book. I won't do it any more.'

'OK,' I said again, not quite believing what I was hearing.

'I didn't like it when you fell. Every time I close my eyes I see it,' she explained, her voice wobbly and full of remorse.

'Forget about it, Alex,' I said, 'it wasn't your fault. It was an accident. I just skidded on the wet decking.'

'At last! A simple explanation from Miss Miller!

Hurrah!' Mr Sharkey said melodramatically. 'Alex, as you have said your piece, if you want to return to After School club, I think that would be OK,' he told her. 'If that's all right with you, Mrs Fryston?'

'Of course,' Mrs Fryston agreed.

Alex, clearly relieved, stood up to go, passing Jolene as she did so. 'See you later, Alex,' Jolene said.

Alex shook her head, not looking at her at all. 'No. I don't want to,' she said quietly. 'We're not friends any more—you're scary.'

I have seen many expressions on Jolene's face over the last few days but I had never seen the one she wore as Alex left. It was as if she had been totally crushed. Any other time, any other person, I'd have felt really bad, but not today. I wasn't that much of a sucker.

No one else seemed to have heard Alex's parting comment—the grown-ups were bringing each other up to date with what had gone on in After School club during Mrs Fryston's absence and Sammie was head-down, staring at the carpet. I turned my attention from Jolene to the girl who had tried to rescue me from her, wondering, dimly, why she was involved at all, really.

'Are you OK?' I whispered, looking up at Sammie. 'You seem upset.'

'Oh, Brody, you look so horrible,' she sniffed.

'Hey, it's like having a face-lift, only cheaper,' I quipped.

But Sammie would not let me cheer her up. She began with the waterworks again. Mrs Fryston broke off her conversation with Mr Sharkey and addressed her. 'Why don't you go back to your film-making for the last part, Sammie? You're singing a duet with Sam, aren't you?'

'No,' Sammie said firmly, 'I'm not leaving Brody. I'm on duty.'

'What do you mean?' Mr Sharkey asked.

'It's private!' she said haughtily, sniffing back tears fiercely and glaring at Jolene.

Mr Sharkey looked at me as if for an explanation but I was as clueless as he was. Mrs Fryston bent down to talk to Sammie. 'Would you like a minute alone with Brody? Would that help?'

'Yes,' Sammie agreed instantly.

'Brody? Is that OK with you?'

I nodded, feeling Jolene's eyes following us as we stepped into the corridor. 'So,' I said, 'what gives?'

Sammie feigned interest in a display of pastel drawings on the notice-board, then looked at me with huge, shiny eyes. 'I'm sorry, Brody!' she sobbed. 'I

89

was meant to be on duty, minding you, and look what happened.'

'What do you mean "minding" me?'

'You know,' she sniffled, now resorting to wiping her nose with the back of her sleeve, 'minding  you, . . . like a minder does . . . like Kevin Costner did to Whitney Houston in that film.'

'Film? You mean *The Bodyguard*? Oh,' I said, as the penny dropped, 'oh! Is that why you're always waiting for me when I come to After School club?'

She nodded hard.

'I thought you were stalking me!'

She looked at me alarmed. 'No!' she cried. 'I was protecting you against stalkers and assassins and things. That was the whole point! Just till you got inside the mobile. I knew I wouldn't be needed inside.'

'But why?'

'Because all famous people have minders and I thought I could be yours. An' I wanted to pay you back.'

'For what?'

She glanced down at her feet. 'For what happened before.'

'Before?' I was really confused.

' . . . when you were so nice to me after I nicked your sponsor money.'

'Oh that,' I said, dragging my mind back to something that had happened so long ago I'd almost forgotten, 'that's ancient history.'

Sammie's face crumpled. 'It's not ancient history to me! You could have dobbed me in but you never. You were magic. I would never have settled into After School club if you hadn't been so nice. That's when I decided I'd pay you back one day but I didn't have nothing to give you, so I thought of the minding thing, cos it wouldn't cost nothing, then . . . then I made a fatal error that minders must never do.'

'What was that?' I said.

'I made the mistake of letting the enemy get close to you because I was fooled into thinking she was your friend. That's why I never stood outside this week and that's why the first time I was needed, I was rubbish! I fell for the oldest trick in the book.' Her shoulders heaved again and I reached out and gave her a massive hug.

'Oh, Sammie, you weren't rubbish. You were miles better than Kevin Costner, who's a real nice guy, by the way.'

But Sammie refused to be mollified. 'I hope Mrs Fryston bans that Jolene—no offence, Brody—I mean, I know she's family and all but she shouldn't be allowed to get away with shoving us around like that. She's a nutter. I haven't said nothing yet but—'

'Sammie,' I said, whispering urgently, 'I did fall. I missed the handrail, OK. If it hadn't been raining and slippery I'd have been fine.'

'No you wouldn't—'

'I would. Sammie, please, I would!'

'If you say so,' she mumbled reluctantly.

'I do.'

She gave her nose a final wipe on the back of her sleeve and shrugged. 'I suppose I'd better get back to Sam. You can't sing "It Takes Two, Baby" on your own.'

'No, you can't.'

As she turned to leave, Sammie glanced at the half-open door to Mr Sharkey's office and said loudly, 'If she starts again, though, I'll bash her in, and that's a promise, that is.'

Chapter Seventeen

No one questioned my version of the incident and it was treated as an accident. We were all given a warning about not going out of bounds, especially in wet weather, and Mrs Fryston filled in her form and Mr Sharkey got back to his paperwork and Jolene and Sammie and I returned to After School club for the last, long hour. The students had already left and packed away all the equipment. The others marvelled at my cuts and grazes and Reggie wanted details about how long the needle had been, then started telling everyone about the time he'd fallen off his bike and his shin bone had come right through the skin and even the surgeon had thrown up at the sight of it. It was easy to see the kind of films he'd be producing when he got older.

I didn't look at Jolene at all. So far she hadn't said a word to me and I decided she could take a hike. If she could do this to someone and not even say sorry, then we were through. I'd be like Kiersten was with her—polite but remote—which was still more than she deserved.

Kiersten was late. She came in all flustered from a lousy journey full of 'ridiculous' roadworks and 'crazy' lorry drivers and then she saw me and nearly dropped on the floor. After a long, long talk with Mrs Fryston she hustled Jolene and me to the car and set off for the station. 'You'd better stay in the car and wait, honey. No way are you standing on the platform tonight in this wind,' she told me.

That was not a problem.

The problem was, Jolene stayed too.

We sat side by side, separated by perspex cubes and silence. As sure as eggs was eggs I wasn't going to talk

to her, so I tried to distract myself, making up mnemonics for the car registration parked in front. MMS. Mini Macaroni Shapes. Minnie Mouse Sucks. My Mouth Stings.

'You don't have to worry. I'll tell him the truth,' Jolene suddenly announced. I jumped, having been used to the silence and not expecting her to break it.

'Who?' I said.

'Grandad Jake. I'll tell him I pushed you. I won't try and get out of it. I'm not a coward. You don't have to protect me.'

'I'm not trying to.'

'Good—cos I don't need you to. I always own up.'

'I don't want you to own up.'

'Why not? I would, if it was the other way round.'

I scowled at her. 'But it's not the other way round, is it? And it's the least you can do.'

She gave me one of her famous sidelong glances. 'I didn't mean to . . . to mess your face up like that,' she muttered.

'Gee, that's not some kind of apology, is it? Anyone get that on tape?' I snapped. I surprised myself at how much anger I was venting but I didn't care. I really didn't care.

'I didn't mean to—'

'Didn't mean to? Just what did you expect to happen when you pushed so hard?'

'Nothing. I never think that far ahead. That's the problem.'

'It sure is. Even your new best friend doesn't want to know you any more.'

She mumbled something.

'What?'

'I'm getting some help for it after the holidays. A child phsycholy-whatsit,' she said, a little more clearly.

'Psychologist?'

'Yeah—one of them. I'm top of the list in our school for anger management lessons.'

'Go figure.'

'I don't like being like this, you know—always in trouble. I can't help it. I get all worked up and then my head fills up with black and I can't even remember what happens, it's all a blur.'

Her voice trembled and I knew she was fighting hard not to cry. Jolene the tough-nut had been replaced by Jolene the . . . well . . . kind of sad. She looked small and lonely and I believed her. I believed she didn't like being like that.

All the anger I had built up since the argument drained away. What was the point of staying mad with her? She was just a mixed-up kid and she had apologized, in her own way. It left me feeling sad, too. 'I wish . . . I wish you'd just told me you were mad at me about what I did when you arrived—you know— with your mom. We could have avoided all this.'

'Yeah, well . . .'

I swallowed hard and my own voice dropped. 'All I ever wanted was to be your friend,' I told her.

There was a long pause, as Jolene considered what I'd said. 'That was never going to happen,' she said finally and I had to admire her for that. Jolene was always honest. Plus it was true. Jolene hadn't clicked with me, not like she had with Alex and you can't force people to get along if they don't click, any more than you can prevent people getting along who do. I'd just got off to a bad start with Jolene and made things worse by trying to keep her and Alex apart. Funny how a bad experience can make things so much clearer. She still shouldn't have pushed me, though!

We sat in silence again, both lost in our thoughts. The windows of the car were steamed up and I wound down the one on my side to let in the cold evening air. In the distance, I could see a train slowly pulling in on to the platform. 'Jake's here,' I said.

'Canny,' Jolene mumbled.

Chapter Eighteen

In Piccollino's, Dad gently tipped my chin first one way, then the other. 'You poor kid! I wish I'd been there for you. No permanent damage though, hinny. Nothing a little airbrushing can't sort out, eh?'

'I guess.'

He'd been pretty calm about my accident but what could he do, anyhow—these things happen, right? As long as Jolene played along, everything would be fine.

'We'll put some witch hazel on those scratches when we get home,' Kiersten added.

Dad requested a look at my tooth. I glanced

quickly at Jolene, who had her eyes glued on the cruet set, and showed him. He grimaced immediately in the same way he had at Sammie's headband that time. 'Oh, what? I've a good mind to sue the pants off that After School club.'

'Jake, don't!' I said in alarm. He just might, knowing him.

'Relax, Brody! Just kidding!' He grinned. 'Though if it had happened a week ago I would not be feeling so magnanimous; but as it is, I have this tiny gem with me to cheer you up!' He winked at Mom and produced a flat envelope which he slid across to me. Inside was one of the pictures he'd taken of me on Jacob's Well Road. It was one where I was slumped against the wall, hands behind my back, looking away from the camera and with one DM crossed over the other. 'That's the image you'll be seeing on every bus stop and every hoarding from one end of the country to the next!' he declared. 'The designers chose it, not me—not one iota of favouritism was involved in the choosing process.'

'That was the one with the edge, then?' I smiled, feeling proud.

He nodded. 'That was the one. Miller and Miller on a roll. What a team, eh?' I smiled widely at him and he smiled widely back. When it came to work, we always clicked.

Mom leaned across and gave Jake a massive kiss on the cheek. 'That's wonderful! It means you can stop being such a grumpy old boot!'

'Hey! Less of the old!' Dad protested.

My tooth was beginning to throb. The anaesthetic had worn off and I didn't feel hungry. Part of me was a little nervous that if I bit down on my new temporary tooth by accident, it would crumble into my plate. Jolene didn't have much appetite, either. She frowned at her menu suspiciously. 'The carbonara's good,' I told her.

'I want my mam,' she mumbled.

'Your mam? I don't see her anywhere on the menu. Try the bolognese instead—it's less chewy,' Jake joked.

'Don't tease, Jake,' Kiersten said, looking concernedly at Jolene. 'Are you OK, honey? You look peaky.'

'I want my mam. I want to go home.'

Jake reached out a hand and touched Jolene lightly on the arm. 'Hey, lighten up, Jolene. We're celebrating. And listen, I'm not going back to work for a few days—I thought you, me, and bruised-up Brody here could take tomorrow off and go to the cinema or something? What do you say?'

I stared at him. I didn't want a day off tomorrow. I wanted to finish filming with Reggie. Kiersten got into a conversation with Jolene and I tugged Jake on the sleeve.

'Jake, I have to finish my project tomorrow.'

'What? And miss a day out with your old man? Never! It's not as if you're missing school. Anyway,' he said, eyeing my face, 'those scratches might be worth a couple of shots—the street urchin look, know what I mean?'

I felt my stomach clench as I prepared to turn him down. 'Thanks, but I don't want to miss After School club tomorrow. It's important.'

He looked at me and shrugged. 'OK—I'll go bug your mother at the gallery and take her to the cinema instead.'

And that was it. That was the first time I'd stood up to my dad and nothing happened. He didn't bust my chops. He didn't disown me. He didn't say I was turning out to be a disappointment just like Claire. He just shrugged. I felt so relieved, until I remembered he was on a high from finishing his project. The real tester would be if I asked for a Coke. Imogen was approaching. Would I dare? I mean, my tooth was gone, right? There was no enamel to save, was there?

But I never got that far. Kiersten was frowning at Jake, telling him something.

'What?' Jake asked.

'My mam's at home. I want to go back,' Jolene said slowly and clearly.

'What do you mean? I thought she wasn't back until Saturday?' Jake asked.

Jolene sighed hard at having to repeat what she'd already told Kiersten. 'I phoned home this afternoon from Mr Sharkey's office. I didn't expect anyone to answer but Keith did and he told me they'd come back early cos they got bored. Mam was out shopping but I'll bet she'll be in now, if you phone her to come and get me.'

She looked at her grandad eagerly and he knew she wouldn't let it drop. He ran his fingers through his hair and sighed. When Imogen arrived to take our order, he shook his head apologetically. 'Forget it,' he said, 'we'll take a raincheck.'

Chapter Nineteen

It turned out to be true. Jake phoned Claire's house as soon as we got in and she answered and admitted they had come home early from Euro Disney but they hadn't called because they didn't want to interrupt Jolene's holiday with us. Nor could they come for Jolene because their car had been broken into while they were away and it wouldn't be fixed until Saturday. Jolene became so distraught when she heard that, Jake promised he'd take her to Washington in the morning, though he told Mom who told me that Claire didn't sound too thrilled about it. 'Weird, isn't it? Anyone would think she didn't want her daughter back. I don't understand it—Jolene's such a cutie, really.'

At night-time, I knocked on Jolene's bedroom door

and asked if I could come in. She didn't reply but I went in anyway. She was sitting on the edge of her bed, ramming her few possessions into her red Sunderland bag. She looked up at me, her face content. 'I'm going home tomorrow,' she said.

'I know.'

'I can't wait.'

'I can see that.'

She glanced at me. 'Did your mam put any of that stuff on your face yet?'

'The witch hazel? No, not yet.'

'I hope it gets better soon.'

It was odd, but I think she had already forgotten who'd done it.

I looked around, not sure why I had come but I just felt I couldn't let her leave without some sort of final ending. Plus there was something a little fishy about this whole 'just got back from Euro Disney' story. 'I didn't know you'd phoned home from Mr Sharkey's office?' I began.

She shrugged. 'Oh yeah—I asked him if I could when he was marching us across the playground. I thought he was going to chuck me out anyway—I'm always being excluded from places—and I thought I'd rather go straight home than . . .'

'Than face After School club tomorrow.'

She shrugged before continuing. 'Well, everyone hates me there now—there's no point in going.'

'Yes, but if you explain about the black—'

But she wasn't interested in that. 'I phoned Nana first but she was out, then I called home, just in case she'd gone round there to clean up . . .'

'I thought your nana was in hospital?'

'Oh, she's out now and miles better.'

I looked closely at her and I just knew she was lying. 'She was never in hospital, was she?'

'She was!'

'And they never went to Euro Disney, did they?'

'Who?'

'Claire and Darryl? They never went.'

Jolene bit her lip. 'Course they did. They went on Space Mountain and everything.'

'No they didn't! You're fibbing. I can tell because you're so lame at it!'

'All right, I am,' she said in a small voice. 'They never went away anywhere but Mam said she couldn't face a week of me arguing with Jack and Keith and Grandma said she was fed up of having me in the holidays and why couldn't Grandad Jake do his turn for once? Mam thought Grandad wouldn't have me if she didn't make up something extreme. That's why she dumped me on your doorstep—she knew she couldn't keep making up details about flights and stuff when they asked. She's a rubbish liar, like me.'

I sighed hard. Poor Jolene. 'I didn't know we were such a screwed-up family,' I said.

'Yours might be, mine isn't,' she stated. I wanted to tell her that my family was her family and we were all screwed up together but I knew she'd see that as a fake thing to say so I sat on the edge of her bed and passed her a pair of socks.

Chapter Twenty

Jake dropped me off at After School club next morning before taking Jolene home. Jolene and I kept it casual, just saying 'see you' to each other when I got out of the car. I guess we didn't have much to say to each other really—everything had been cleared up last night. As I reached across for my bag, she handed me an envelope. 'Will you give that to Alex for me? It's got my address in and everything,' she said.

Our eyes met. 'I'll try,' I said, 'but I can't promise you anything.' I took the envelope then went round to Dad's side. He wound the window down and leaned out to give me a big hug.

'Take care of yourself, hinny, I'll see you tonight.'

'OK.'

'I'm sorry I'm having to do this—I'd got some quality time planned, but never mind.'

'Give it to Jolene—she needs it,' I told him, 'and find out what potato chips she likes.'

He looked at me kind of strangely but I just waved goodbye and headed for the mobile. I had a film to finish with my buddies.

Epilogue

The last two days of film-making went so fast, I barely thought about Jolene at all. Isn't that terrible? I settled right back in as if nothing had happened, unless I happened to pass a mirror. That's what I like about After School club—nobody makes a fuss but you know they all care. Weird, isn't it? I'd been thinking all this time that I didn't have any special friends at Zetland Avenue when it turned out everybody was my special friend—Sammie, Reggie, Brandon, Lloyd, Sam—even Mrs Fryston and Mr Sharkey. Sharkey and Fryston make a good team, don't they? I have a feeling Mr Sharkey knew all along about what happened out there on the steps but he was waiting to hear my angle first before he took any action. That makes good leadership, in my book.

Anyhow, we finished the films and premièred them in front of the parents on Friday afternoon. The students set up a mini Oscar ceremony. *Reggie Riding Hood* didn't win the best foreign language category but it won best costume and best screen kiss. Yep, that's what I said. Best kiss. OK, I'd better tell you about that one, though it was pretty embarrassing at the time, especially as Kiersten and Jake were in the audience.

Thursday afternoon we were on set, OK, recording the main part, where Reggie Riding Hood is giving it the 'what big eyes you've got' routine. I was sitting up in bed (two chairs pushed together with a rug over my knees), adjusting my bonnet because it was too tight for my springy hair, when Reggie delivered the 'What big eyes tha's got, our gran,' bit, then smirked and leaned in close.

'All the better for seeing you with, Reggie Riding 'Ud,' I said in my best Yorkshire accent, which still had a long way to go.

Reggie leaned in closer. 'My, what a messed-up face tha's got, our gran—it looks like roadkill,' he yelled.

That wasn't in the script but I just scowled at him in a wolf-like manner and said, 'All the better for . . . ' Then I halted because I couldn't think of how to end it. Then, before I knew what was happening, he bent down and said, 'I'd better kiss it better for thee!' and he pecked me lightly on the cheek. Lloyd, who was on camera at the time, started giggling and when you watch the film you can tell because it goes all shaky at that point. Anyway, afterwards Reggie said, 'I suppose I could go out with you; but keep the sloppy stuff to a minimum,' so I said, 'Fine, it's a deal.' Just for the record, Reggie is now my boyfriend but dating in Year Six just means we sit together on the computers at After School club and we get teased a lot in Mrs Platini's.

What else happened? Well, Sammie went back to her guard-post on the steps, watching out for stalkers and assassins attacking me from all corners of the school yard. Only now she looks the part because I gave her the shades that Jake said fell off the back of a Porsche. She was *so* delighted. Sammie has a birthday coming up soon and I'm getting her a microphone headset to go with them and before you ask, yes, I replaced Gemma's headband—three times over. I made Jake pay for them too—I told him he had no right doing that to people's property and he actually agreed. I'm getting braver at telling him when I don't want to do stuff and so far it's been OK, just like in the restaurant. I'll never get to the real heated exchanges with him, though, it's not my style. Besides, we're so busy working on the autumn/winter collection for Funky Punk we don't have time to argue.

As for Alex, she took the part of Granny and kept her promise about being nicer to Brandon. She even bought him some sweets from the tuck shop—all green, of course; Brandon only eats one kind of colour candy just as he only reads one title of book.

I don't know what she did about Jolene's letter—she never said and I never asked. I reckon she did Jolene a big favour, though, by telling her she didn't want to be her friend any more. I think it shocked Jolene into thinking about her actions much more than breaking my tooth did.

Last I heard, Jolene was doing OK but it's difficult getting news from people who don't really communicate. Still, Jolene knows my number—she's free to call any time.

Alex is up next with her story. I really don't know much about her, except she isn't as annoying as I first thought she was.

Do You Know a Brody?

Have you got a friend who reminds you of Brody? Perhaps someone you know is interested in modelling? Or maybe they've got a strange family tree? Or do you have a funny story about acting in or writing a play?

If you have a story, send it to us at the After School Club website. We'll print the best stories and find out who is the biggest Brody of all!

www.oup.com/uk/children/afterschoolclub

After School Club

starring Sammie . . .

My life's a mess!

My dad's left home, all my mum cares about is going clubbing, and my sisters are a complete pain in the you-know-where.

As if that's not bad enough, I've just told a big fat lie, and I don't know how I'm going to get out of it. How would you get £100 by Monday?

At least things are normal at the After School Club, well, so far, anyway . . .

ISBN 0 19 275247 2

starring Alex . . .

It's just so unfair!

Mum's so busy with all her committees and stuff that she never has time for me. And now everyone's saying I've got an attitude problem – well, thanks a bunch.

I think they must have the wrong girl – I'm just misunderstood, an angel really. But still, I'll show them what they can do with their opinions. If they want attitude, they've got it.

I thought mum being a helper at After School Club would be great – but even that's turning into a nightmare . . .

ISBN 0 19 275249 9